# Raisin and Grape

by Tom Amico and James Proimos
illustrated by Andy Snair

Dial Books
for Young Readers

This is my grandpa.
He's a raisin.
He's coming to visit me today.

This is me.

When I get old,
I'll be a raisin like Grandpa.
And I'll probably be a
king or something.

Grandpa will never be a grape again.
"You couldn't pay me to be a grape again,"
he says.
Being a raisin means you have a lot of wrinkles.
Grandpa must have a kazillion.
Awesome!

It's Grandpa's birthday. He's had a lot of birthdays. Grandpa's so old that he's been allowed to cross the big street for more years than I can count.

I'm not allowed to cross the big street yet. Grandpa says, "You know how they make grape juice?" I ask, "How?" And he says, "They just let some grapes cross the street without holding their grandpa's hand."

Today Grandpa is taking me to the park.

He walks slow. I'm fast.

But Grandpa's a good yeller. So I come back to him.

Grandpa tells long stories on the way to the park. I can only listen short. But I like the parts I do listen to. Grandpa has a kazillion stories. That's one for each wrinkle.

Grandpa says we make a good team. When I climb a tree, Grandpa gets nervous. "Come on down, squirt," he says, and I do. "If I weren't here to be nervous, you might climb too high and fall."

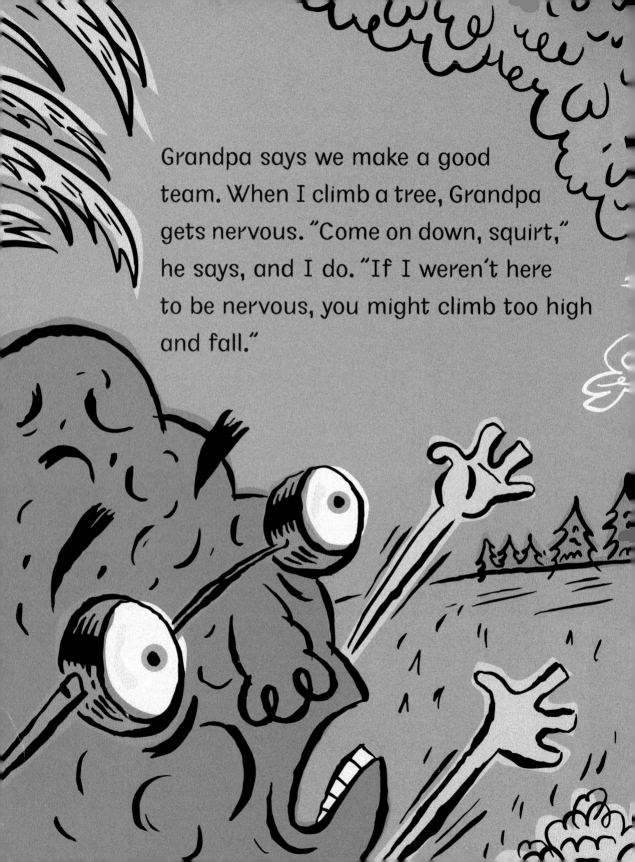

Grandpa teaches me about
life's ups and downs

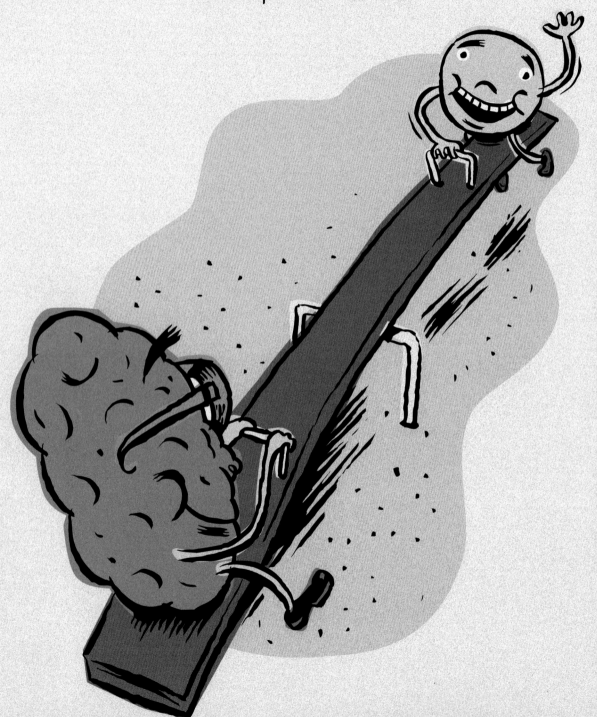

and taking pride in your work.

He reminds me to
stop and smell the flowers.
I would forget that without him.

I stop to smell my armpits.
"Fresh and clean," I say.
"Very funny," Grandpa says.

When the prune who talks too much sits next to Grandpa, I say, "Time to go, Grandpa. I need a nap." I pull his hand and Grandpa whispers to me, "You saved me again."

On the way home from the park Grandpa says,
"When I was a grape, I was just like you."

And then I say, "When I'm a raisin, I want
to be just like YOU—except king!"

And then we hug.
Sometimes a little too tight.

For the loveliest raisin, Salvatrice
—J.P.

For the sweetest grape, Renata
—T.A.

For Lucy and Little Joe
—A.S.

DIAL BOOKS FOR YOUNG READERS
A division of Penguin Young Readers Group
Published by The Penguin Group
Penguin Group (USA) Inc., 375 Hudson Street, New York, NY 10014, U.S.A.
Penguin Group (Canada), 90 Eglinton Avenue East, Suite 700, Toronto, Ontario, Canada M4P2Y3
(a division of Pearson Penguin Canada Inc.)
Penguin Books Ltd, 80 Strand, London WC2R ORL, England
Penguin Ireland, 25 St. Stephen's Green, Dublin 2, Ireland
(a division of Penguin Books Ltd)
Penguin Group (Australia), 250 Camberwell Road, Camberwell, Victoria 3124, Australia
(a division of Pearson Australia Group Pty Ltd)
Penguin Books India Pvt Ltd, 11 Community Centre,
Panchsheel Park, New Delhi - 110 017, India
Penguin Group (NZ), Cnr Airborne and Rosedale Roads, Albany, Auckland 1310,
New Zealand (a division of Pearson New Zealand Ltd)
Penguin Books (South Africa) (Pty) Ltd, 24 Sturdee Avenue,
Rosebank, Johannesburg 2196, South Africa
Penguin Books Ltd, Registered Offices: 80 Strand, London WC2R ORL, England

Designed by Jasmin Rubero
Text set in Green Terror
Manufactured in China on acid-free paper
1 3 5 7 9 10 8 6 4 2

Library of Congress Cataloging-in-Publication Data
Amico, Tom.
Raisin and Grape / by Tom Amico and James Proimos ; pictures by Andy Snair.
p.  cm.
Summary: A young grape and his grandfather, a wrinkly raisin,
enjoy spending time together telling jokes and going to the park.
ISBN 0-8037-3091-8
[1. Grandfathers—Fiction. 2. Grapes—Fiction. 3. Raisins—Fiction.] I. Proimos, James.
II. Snair, Andy, ill. III. Title.
PZ7.A5163Rai 2006   2005000338